DRAGON SLAYERS' ACADEMY™ 4

A WEDDING FOR WIGLAF?

By Kate McMullan
Cover illustration by Stephen Gilpin
Illustrated by Bill Basso

Grosset & Dunlap
An Imprint of Penguin Group (USA) Inc.

30567 2188

For Audrey Kubetin
—KM

GROSSET & DUNLAP
Published by the Penguin Group
Penguin Group (USA) Inc., 375 Hudson Street, New York, New York 10014, USA
Penguin Group (Canada), 90 Eglinton Avenue East, Suite 700,
Toronto, Ontario M4P 2Y3, Canada (a division of Pearson Penguin Canada Inc.)
Penguin Books Ltd., 80 Strand, London WC2R 0RL, England
Penguin Group Ireland, 25 St. Stephen's Green, Dublin 2, Ireland
(a division of Penguin Books Ltd.)
Penguin Group (Australia), 250 Camberwell Road, Camberwell, Victoria 3124, Australia
(a division of Pearson Australia Group Pty. Ltd.)
Penguin Books India Pvt. Ltd., 11 Community Centre,
Panchsheel Park, New Delhi—110 017, India
Penguin Group (NZ), 67 Apollo Drive, Rosedale, Auckland 0632, New Zealand
(a division of Pearson New Zealand Ltd.)
Penguin Books (South Africa) (Pty.) Ltd., 24 Sturdee Avenue,
Rosebank, Johannesburg 2196, South Africa

Penguin Books Ltd., Registered Offices: 80 Strand, London WC2R 0RL, England

Cover illustration by Stephen Gilpin.

Library of Congress Control Number: 98041532

ISBN 978-0-448-43111-6   10 9 8 7 6 5 4 3 2 1

ALWAYS LEARNING   PEARSON

Chapter 1

Wiglaf pushed his carrot-colored hair off his sweaty brow. It was a hot spring day. Coach Plungett had given his class a break to get a drink. Wiglaf and the other students stood in line at the well in the castle yard, waiting for a turn with the dipper.

Coach leaned against the well. "I've killed many a dragon, lads," he said. "Ah, yes...but I'll never forget the first. You never do. Hotblaze was his name. The beast spewed flames so hot they melted my helmet. Burned my hair off, too. Been bald as a potato ever since. But that didn't stop me. I drew my sword like a manly man! I jabbed Hotblaze in his left flank. Or...was it his right?" Coach pushed back his brown, pageboy-style wig. He scratched his hairless head, trying to think.

Wiglaf hoped Coach wouldn't go on and on, telling how Hotblaze met his end. Blood-and-guts stories always made him feel sick to his stomach.

"Wiglaf!" someone called.

Wiglaf turned. He saw his friend Angus hurrying across the castle yard.

"Uncle Mordred wants to see you in his office right away!" Angus yelled.

Me? Wiglaf pointed to himself.

"Go on, lad," Coach told Wiglaf. "You can get the homework from Torblad."

"Nice knowing you, Wiglaf," Torblad scoffed.

Wiglaf trotted off. He was glad to get out of class. But he hated to think why he was being summoned by the hot-tempered headmaster of Dragon Slayers' Academy.

Mordred was not fond of Wiglaf. For Wiglaf had, quite by accident, killed two dragons, Gorzil and Seetha. But he had not brought Mordred any of their dragon gold.

Wiglaf caught up with Angus. "What does Mordred want?" he asked. The two began hurrying toward the old castle that housed DSA.

Angus shrugged. "Uncle Mordred didn't say. But he wasn't angry. In fact, he seemed rather...jolly."

"Jolly?" Wiglaf exclaimed. That was a new one. Mordred was never jolly.

The boys ran all the way to Mordred's office. Angus knocked on the door.

"Enter!" boomed a voice.

The boys entered. They found Mordred standing next to his desk, reading a copy of

The Medieval Times. He wore a red velvet tunic with golden dragons stitched on it.

"Ah, Wiglaf!" Mordred put down his newspaper. "Back to work, Angus," he added, never taking his violet eyes from Wiglaf. "I don't pay you half a penny a year to stand around gawking!"

"No, Uncle," Angus said. He went back to polishing the headmaster's big black boots.

"Ah, Wiglaf!" Mordred exclaimed again. "How are you feeling, my boy? Fit as a fiddle, I hope?"

"Yes, thank you, sir," Wiglaf answered. He wondered why the headmaster had asked. Mordred was not one to worry about the health of his students. Quite the opposite, in fact.

"And your pet pig," Mordred went on. "Is Daisy happy living out in the henhouse?"

"Very happy, sir," Wiglaf answered.

It surprised him that Mordred knew about

Daisy. He had brought his dear pig to school with him from his home in Pinwick. He wondered if Mordred also knew that Daisy was under a wizard's spell. She could speak—in Pig Latin.

"Is Frypot feeding you enough lumpen pudding?" Mordred asked.

"More than enough, sir," Wiglaf said.

"Excuse me, Uncle Mordred," Angus said. He held up a boot. "Is this shiny enough for you?"

"You must be joking!" Mordred yelled. "Put some elbow grease into it, nephew!"

Angus sighed and went back to polishing.

"Now, about clothes, Wiglaf," Mordred said. "My sister Lobelia will order you a new tunic. And fine new britches, too."

"Clothes?" Wiglaf said. "But I have no money! I cannot pay for new clothes."

"Worry not, my boy," Mordred said, still smiling. "I shall pay for everything!"

Wiglaf gasped. Now he understood. Mordred had lost his mind!

The DSA headmaster was a famous penny-pincher. He never spent a cent if he could help it. He would never, in a million years, pay for anything for anybody else. Especially not for Wiglaf.

There was a sudden knock on the door.

"Enter!" Mordred said.

The door flew open. Erica ran into the office. Erica dressed as a boy so she could go to DSA. Everyone there called her Eric. Wiglaf was the only student who knew that she was a girl. And a royal one at that. She was none other than Princess Erica, daughter of Queen Barb and King Ken.

"Sir!" Erica cried. "Come quickly! Torblad fell into the moat. And he cannot swim!"

"Torblad, eh?" Mordred scratched his chin thoughtfully. "I wonder if he is all paid up.

Let me check my records." He opened a worn leather book. On the cover, it said:

MORDRED'S MONEY

Private! Keep Out! No Peeking! I Mean It!

"Hmmm. Just as I thought," the headmaster muttered. "Torblad owes me for two semesters." Mordred jumped up suddenly. "Egad!" he cried. "If he drowns, I'll never see a penny of it! Wait here, Wiglaf. I'll be back!" The headmaster raced from the room. Erica raced after him.

Wiglaf turned to Angus. "Your uncle has gone mad!" he said. "Why else would he offer to buy me new clothes?"

"Oh, he has something up his sleeve," Angus said. "You can be sure of that." He put down the boot he was polishing. He picked up Mordred's copy of *The Medieval Times.* "Let's see if Dragon Stabbers' Prep beat Knights-R-Us in the jousting match," he said.

"Wait," said Wiglaf. "What's this on the front page?" Together, the boys read the headline story.

BELCHEENA WORTH BILLIONS
Super-Rich Princess Seeks Husband
EAST ARMPITTSIA Wednesday, June 8—

Years ago, Princess Belcheena's heart was broken. The love of her life rode off, never to be seen again. The princess shut herself up in her tower in Mildew Palace. She comforted herself by counting her gold. She has great mountains of it, so counting it took a long time. But last week, she finished. Now the princess has come out into the world again. And she is looking for a husband.

"I have over twelve billion in gold coins," the princess told reporters on Monday. "Now all I need is a special someone to help me spend it. Princes seek wives all the time," she added. "Why shouldn't a princess seek a husband?"

There are three things the princess is looking for in her future groom. He must be a dragon slayer.

He must be a redhead. And his name must begin with Princess Belcheena's favorite letter of the alphabet—W.

"The matchmaker who finds me the right husband will get a pot of gold," the princess promised.

Angus whistled. "Belcheena is loaded!"

"I wonder why her true love rode away," Wiglaf said.

Just then the door swung open. Mordred was back. His hair and his tunic dripped with foul-smelling moat water.

"Torblad is saved," he growled. "But he had better pay up soon. Or I'll throw the little rotter back into the moat myself."

Mordred glanced at Angus and Wiglaf. "Ah, you've seen the paper!" he said. "I guess my little surprise is out of the bag. Eh, Wiglaf?"

"Your surprise, sir?" Wiglaf asked.

"Yes, my boy," Mordred said happily. "You are about to get married!"

Chapter 2

xcuse me, sir?" Wiglaf managed. "I don't think I heard you right."

"You...are...about...to...get...married," Mordred said again.

Wiglaf looked over his shoulder. Mordred had to be speaking to someone behind him.

But there was no one behind him.

"You cannot mean Wiglaf," Angus said.

"Oh, but I do!" Mordred picked up the paper. "Belcheena says her husband must be a dragon slayer. And Wiglaf has slain two dragons."

"But only by accident, sir!" Wiglaf cried. "Surely the princess wants a husband who slew his dragons on purpose."

"Fiddle-faddle," Mordred said. He glanced at the paper again. "Belcheena wants a redheaded husband. And you, Wiglaf, are a redhead."

"My hair is orange, sir," Wiglaf pointed out.

"Close enough," Mordred growled. "Next you will tell me that Wiglaf does not begin with *W!*"

"No, sir," Wiglaf said miserably.

"Well then!" Mordred boomed. "It looks as if I shall be a matchmaker! And I shall get the pot of gold!" He rubbed his hands together. "Ha! I knew there was an easier way to get rich than sending half-witted boys out to bring me dragon gold!"

Mordred glanced at the sundial on his desk. "Off with you now, Wiglaf," he said. "Come back after supper tonight. Lobelia will be here then. And we'll make plans for your wedding!"

Wiglaf fell to his knees. "I am a peasant!" he

cried. "My twelve brothers smell bad, for my father thinks bathing causes madness! My—"

"Say no more, Wiglaf," Mordred cut him off. "I understand what you are telling me."

"Oh, do you, sir?" Wiglaf cried happily.

"Certainly," Mordred said. "You don't want to invite your family to the wedding."

"Uh...that is not exactly what I meant, sir," Wiglaf said. "I was trying to explain how very unfit I am to mar...mar..." He could not bring himself to say the awful word! "How unfit I am for a princess," he said at last.

Mordred frowned. "You are a redheaded dragon slayer named Wiglaf. You are exactly what the princess wants. I shall make this known to her. And I shall get the pot of gold. I wonder," he added dreamily, "just how big a pot it is?"

Mordred stared into space, imagining his pot of gold. The boys quietly left his office. They headed for Scrubbing Class.

"Can your uncle really make me get mar... mar..." Try as he might, Wiglaf could not say it! "Can he make me do this thing?" Wiglaf asked.

"He seems to think so," Angus said.

They walked in silence for a while. Then Angus said, "Do not take this the wrong way, Wiglaf. But when the princess sees you, surely she will put a stop to any wedding."

"I hope you're right," Wiglaf said. But he was worried. Mordred was so set on getting that pot of gold.

The boys reached the DSA kitchen. Frypot stood at the door. "Hurry in to class, boys," he called. "You may think Scrubbing is not as exciting as Slaying Class. But wait until you make a kill. It's a mess, what with the dragon guts hanging off your sword and all. Then you'll be glad you took old Frypot's Scrubbing Class."

Wiglaf hurried over to Erica on the far side

of the room. She was scraping burned lumpen pudding from a big pot. *How like Erica to pick the dirtiest pot,* Wiglaf thought. No wonder she always won the Dragon Slayer of the Month medal.

"Wiglaf!" Erica cried when she saw him. "What were you doing in Mordred's office?"

"I'll tell you," Wiglaf whispered. "But first I must ask you something. Do you princesses—"

"Talk not of princesses!" Erica hissed. "If you have breathed a word of my secret, Wiglaf..."

"I have said nothing!" Wiglaf said. "I swear it on my sword!"

"Ha!" Erica scoffed. "That rusty old thing?"

"I shall never tell your secret," Wiglaf said. "But tell me! Do you know Belcheena?"

"Belcheena!" Erica cried.

Several heads turned toward them.

"Shhhh!" Wiglaf whispered. "What is she like?"

"Belcheena doesn't come out of her tower much," Erica said. "But I saw her once at a Princess Talent Contest. That was the day I won first prize in sword fighting! True, only one other princess had entered, but I—"

"What about Belcheena?" Wiglaf put in.

"As I remember, she sang a sad song. 'The Squire of My Desire,' I think. Why do you ask, Wiglaf?"

"There is a story about her in the paper," Wiglaf said. "She is looking for a husband."

"Belcheena is very..." Erica stopped for a moment. "How shall I put it? Belcheena has a very strong personality. I pity the man who marries her."

"Then you may have to pity me!" Wiglaf cried. And he told Erica all that had taken place in Mordred's office.

"I have no wish to marry *anyone*," Wiglaf finished up. "I want to stay here at DSA with my friends. I want to become a knight some-day. I want to travel the kingdom, helping villagers. And saving small, helpless animals—"

"Yes, yes," Erica broke in. "So tell Mordred that you won't marry Belcheena."

"But she has promised a pot of gold to the matchmaker who finds her a redheaded, dragon-slaying, *W*-named husband," Wiglaf said. "And Mordred has his heart set on this pot."

"Ah," Erica said. "Mordred is after her gold, is he? Well then, if I were you, Wiggie, I know what I'd be doing right now."

"What?" Wiglaf cried. "Tell me!"

Erica smiled. "I'd be picking out the perfect spot for my honeymoon!"

Chapter 3

The lumpen pudding that night was even worse than usual. Frypot had burned it to a crisp. But he hacked the blackened glop to pieces and served it anyway.

After supper, Wiglaf felt sick. But he didn't know if it was from the pudding or the thought of getting mar...mar... Oh, he could not even think it! Slowly he made his way to Mordred's office.

Mordred beamed as he let Wiglaf in. "Here he is, Lobelia. The lucky groom!"

Lobelia smiled. She had violet eyes and thick dark hair like Mordred. But there the likeness between brother and sister ended.

Lobelia was thin and known for her high style.

"Sit, Wiglaf," Mordred said.

Wiglaf sat down across from Mordred's desk.

"I have written to Belcheena." Mordred handed Wiglaf a sheet of parchment. "This is a first draft. Read it—quickly! I shall have Brother Dave up in the—oh, what do you call that room in the tower with all the books?"

"The library," Wiglaf said.

"Yes, yes," Mordred said. "Brother Dave up in the library will copy it over. Then I shall send it off to Belcheena."

Wiglaf's hand shook as he held the letter:

Wednesday, June 8

To Her Royal Ri~~ch~~ness Highness,

Princess Bil~~kons~~ Belcheena, Mildew Palace, East Armpittsia

Dear Princess ~~Bil~~ Belcheena:

I have read of your search for a husband. I know

such a ~~boy~~ ~~man~~ ~~twerp~~ person as you describe. He has killed two dragons. His hair is red. His name is *Wiglaf of Pinwick.*

As you can see, he meets all your requirements. So come and marry him. Do not delay. His heart ~~thumps~~ ~~clonks~~ ~~pounds~~ ~~beats~~ pitter-patters with love for you already.

Your number one matchmaker,

Mordred the Marvelous, Headmaster DSA

P.S. Wiglaf is perfect for you. So go ahead and bring along that great big pot of gold.

Wiglaf's heart indeed thumped, clonked, pounded, beat, and pitter-pattered. Not with love. But with fear that this awful thing might really happen!

Lobelia skimmed the letter. "Very nice, Mordie," she said when she finished.

Mordred smiled. He pulled a velvet bell cord hanging on the wall. A DSA student teacher quickly appeared at the door.

"Take this to Brother Dave." Mordred handed him the letter. "Wait while he copies it. Then give the copy to my scout, Yorick. Tell him to deliver it to Mildew Palace tonight."

Tonight! Wiglaf gulped. Things were moving quickly. Way too quickly!

"Now for the wedding plans!" Lobelia held up a list she had made. "The wedding shall take place in the rose garden," she said.

Mordred frowned. "What rose garden?"

"The one I shall plant in the castle yard," Lobelia replied. "I'm thinking red roses to go with the redhead theme. After the wedding, we'll have the feast. Frypot and I planned a menu to go with Belcheena's favorite letter— *W*. We're serving whitefish, Welsh rarebit, wolf chops, weasel tenderloin, wrens and warblers baked in a pie, watermelon, and wine. But Mordie, this will not come cheap."

"Spare no expense!" Mordred said. "A

princess must have a proper wedding. And surely Belcheena will pay for the whole shebang!"

Lobelia nodded. "Now, Wiglaf, you must pick a best man. Your most trusted friend in the world. One to stand by you as you say your vows."

"You should choose someone important," Mordred said. "Someone powerful. Someone...like me."

Wiglaf rolled his eyes. Mordred was the cause of this mess. He would never pick him. Angus and Erica were his good friends. But his most trusted friend in the world? That was his pig, Daisy. Wiglaf almost laughed, thinking what Mordred and Lobelia would say if he suggested that Daisy be in the wedding. A best pig! They would think he had lost his mind!

And suddenly Wiglaf realized that's just what he *would* say! If Mordred and Lobelia thought he was crazy, maybe they would give up trying to make him marry the princess.

"My best friend must stand by me!" Wiglaf declared.

"Fine," Lobelia said. "Just tell me his name. I will have him measured for a new tunic."

"It is a she," Wiglaf said. "My pig, Daisy."

"Your pig? Over my dead body!" Mordred roared.

"Daisy must stand by me!" Wiglaf smiled strangely. He tried to look quite mad.

"I'll roast that pig of yours for the wedding supper!" Mordred roared.

"Stop, Mordie," Lobelia said. "Clearly the pig cannot be the best man. But picture this. Daisy as...the flower girl!"

"Have you lost your mind?" Mordred bellowed.

"Not her, me!" Wiglaf cried. "I'm the one who's lost my mind!"

"Shush!" Lobelia said. "A flower pig has

never been done. It's new. Cutting-edge! What a statement it would make!"

Panic gripped Wiglaf. He had not counted on this! How could Lobelia want a pig in a wedding? He had to do something fast.

"Yes! Here's the statement it would make!" Wiglaf said. And he started oinking like a pig.

"Stop that, Wiglaf," ordered Lobelia. "It would say our lives are connected to the earth. To beasts—the pig. This is such a fine idea," she added. "Perhaps the hens should be in the wedding, too."

"Ooooh! I feel a headache coming on!" Mordred groaned. "All right, Lobelia. Make what plans you will. But I warn you..." He raised one bushy eyebrow. "Don't do a thing that will put a stop to this wedding. For I shall let nothing—*nothing!*—stand between me and that pot of gold!"

Chapter 4

Wiglaf stumbled into the dorm room late that night. But Angus and Erica had waited up for him.

"What happened, Wiggie?" Erica whispered. "Did you talk Mordred out of this crazy idea?"

Wiglaf shook his head. "Mordred wrote Belcheena that he had found the perfect husband for her.... Me!" he wailed. "Yorick is on his way to Mildew Palace with the letter right now!"

"Well, look at the bright side," Angus advised. "You will be very rich."

"What do I care for riches?" Wiglaf moaned.

"You can order the best suit of armor from *The Sir Lancelot Catalog*," Erica pointed out. "And the ruby-handled sword!"

Wiglaf pictured the handsome ruby-handled sword from Erica's catalog. That part didn't sound so bad.

"No more lumpen pudding," Angus said. "And no more Scrubbing Class!"

"I hadn't thought about that," Wiglaf said.

"And someone will wait on you, hand and foot," Erica added. "You'll like that, Wiggie."

Wiglaf smiled. "That's *Prince* Wiggie to you!" Then his smile faded. "But I don't want to get mar... Oh, why did Mordred write that letter?"

"You know..." Angus said thoughtfully. "We, too, can write a letter."

Erica grinned. "Our letter could say how awful Wiglaf of Pinwick really is!"

"Yes!" Wiglaf cried. "Let us write it now!"

Erica ran off to her bunk. She quickly returned with paper and a goose quill pen.

"You write it, Angus." She gave him the supplies. "You have the worst handwriting."

"All right," Angus agreed. He settled himself on the floor. "What shall I write?"

"Dear Princess Belcheena," Wiglaf began. "A greedy matchmaker wrote you of a red-headed dragon slayer, Wiglaf of Pinwick. He wrote that Wiglaf would make you a perfect husband. Nothing could be further from the truth!"

"Let me add a bit," Erica said. And she took over. "You will know Wiglaf when you see him by the handsome wart on the tip of his nose. His lips are always nicely moist, for his drooling keeps them wet. Are you fond of dogs? I ask, for Wiglaf's breath is so like that of a hound. His teeth are artistically arranged. Some lean to the left. Others to the right. Still others lean way out of his mouth."

"Enough about my looks," Wiglaf said quickly.

Erica nodded. "Wiglaf would rather walk a mile on burning coals than marry you," she went on. "But he is a fortune hunter. And you have a fortune. So he shall wed you for your gold." Erica smiled. "That is enough, I think."

Wiglaf took the pen. He signed the letter, "From a True Friend at DSA." He blew on the ink to dry it. Then he rolled the letter up. Erica tied it with a ribbon.

"Let us keep this mar...mar...this thing a secret," Wiglaf suggested. "I have no wish for the other students here to know about it."

"I shan't say a word," Angus promised.

"Me either," Erica said. "I swear it on my genuine Sir Lancelot sword!"

The three friends locked pinkies to seal their promise.

"Maybe Yorick is back from Mildew Palace by now," Erica said. "Let's go see."

They tiptoed out of the dorm. They ran

silently through the hallways and across the castle yard. Wiglaf opened the door to the gatehouse. But it was empty except for a large rock on a pile of straw.

"Too bad," Angus said. "Yorick isn't here."

Suddenly the rock sat up. A hand reached out and slipped off a gray hood.

"Yorick!" Wiglaf exclaimed. "We thought you were a rock."

"That's the idea," Yorick said, getting to his feet. "This is my rock disguise—gray tights, a gray tunic, gray hood. When I spot trouble, I squat down by the side of the road. People take me for a rock and walk on by."

"We have a letter, Yorick," Wiglaf said. "It must be delivered to Mildew Palace right away."

"I just got back from there!" Yorick exclaimed. "I'm not going again so soon. Not on your life."

"I shall pay you a penny," Angus offered.

"No, Angus!" Wiglaf cried. "Your mother gave you that penny for your birthday!"

"It's a small price to pay to keep you from getting married and— oops!" Angus clapped a hand to his mouth.

"Wiglaf's getting married?" Yorick asked.

"Not if I can help it," Wiglaf said quickly. "That's why we need you to take this letter."

Angus gave Yorick the penny. Yorick bit down on it to make sure it was real.

"I'm off!" Yorick took the letter from Wiglaf. He tucked it into his tunic. And he hurried away.

Tomorrow morning, Wiglaf thought, *Princess Belcheena will read this letter. And she will never want to lay eyes on Wiglaf of Pinwick!*

Wiglaf, Angus, and Erica started back across the yard. They had almost reached the castle when a voice called: "Halt! Who goes there?"

Wiglaf froze. So did Angus and Erica.

"Oh, it's you three," the voice said. It belonged to Coach Plungett. "I thought I'd caught a pack of thieves on my watch," Coach said with a chuckle. He put his sword away. "What are you lads doing out here at this time of night?"

"We...uh," Wiglaf began. "We were just..."

"We couldn't sleep," Erica put in.

"Couldn't sleep, eh?" Coach looked up at the starry sky. "I once suffered from sleepless nights," he said. "It was long ago. I couldn't sleep for thinking of my lady love."

"You were in love!" Angus cried. "Yuck!"

Wiglaf smiled. It was funny to think of Coach Plungett in love. And yet...Coach had never married. How had he escaped?

"Excuse me, Coach?" Wiglaf said. "If I may ask—how is it you never mar...mar..."

"Married?" Coach said. "I was a lowly squire and my lady love's father thought I'd never amount to a hill of beans. One night he sent his henchmen to tell me to go. Said they'd stab me full of holes if I returned. There were twenty of them. And only one of me. So I rode off. I thought it best at the time." Coach sighed. "But sometimes I wonder, lads."

Wiglaf sighed, too. Clearly Coach's story was no help to him.

"That's a sad tale, Coach," said Angus.

"'Tis," Coach agreed. "Now go in and get some sleep. I won't be in class for a few days, you know. I'm off to Ratswhiskers to visit my mother. Sir Mort will take over for me. He'll be showing you the Fatal Blow."

"Good night, Coach," the three called. Then they headed for the castle.

Wiglaf had a light heart all day on Thursday. He pictured the princess opening the second letter. And crossing Wiglaf of

Pinwick off her list of possible husbands.

Friday morning, Wiglaf, Erica, and Angus walked into the dining hall for breakfast. Wiglaf caught sight of Mordred. He was running toward him, waving a piece of parchment. The headmaster was smiling broadly. This was not a good sign.

"Princess Belcheena has written back!" Mordred exclaimed as he reached Wiglaf.

Wiglaf's heart began to pound. Something was amiss. He could feel it in his bones.

"Her steward brought her reply this morning," Mordred went on. "Listen to what she says!"

Wiglaf looked nervously around the dining hall. All the boys had stopped eating. They were silent, waiting to hear more.

"*My dear Mordred,*" Mordred read loudly. "*How kind of you to write to let me know that Wiglaf of Pinwick would make me such a fine husband!*"

"Woo! Woo! Woo!" shouted all the boys in the dining hall. "Wiglaf's getting married!"

"Silence!" Mordred roared. His violet eyes flashed with anger. He read on.

"*'I shall gladly come to Dragon Slayers' Academy to meet this redheaded dragon slayer. Please have your best room ready for me.'* Then she says something about even if I have to move out of the best room myself...clean sheets, blah, blah, blah. Let me see..." His eyes traveled down the page. "Ah! *'I shall arrive on Saturday with my ladies-in-waiting, servants, and hangers-on. If Wiglaf is as perfect as you say, we shall be wed the following Saturday. I shall, of course, bring the pot of gold.*

Sincerely,

Princess Belcheena, Mildew Palace.'"

"Let us be wed, Wiglaf, honey!" called a boy.

Wiglaf's face burned hot with shame.

"She'll bring her gold!" Mordred exclaimed.

"That is the main thing. And she will be here tomorrow! Oh, there is much to do!"

Wiglaf tried to think. Belcheena must have sent this letter before she received the second one. Yes, that was it. Surely Mordred would soon get a second letter from Belcheena. And this one would say she was not coming after all.

"We must hurry!" Mordred said over the jeering boys. "We can't have Belcheena backing out of the deal when she lays eyes on you, Wiglaf. Come!" He grabbed Wiglaf's arm. "We must get you to Lobelia right away! She'll teach you manners. Show you how to eat with a knife, the way proper folks do. She'll show you how to bow. And most important, how to kiss the princess's hand."

The last thing Wiglaf heard as Mordred dragged him from the dining hall was boys making loud, juicy kissing sounds.

Chapter 5

"**S**ister!" Mordred cried. He flung Wiglaf into Lobelia's chamber. "Teach this riffraff some manners. And quickly! Belcheena is coming tomorrow. We can't have her refusing to marry the boy because he acts like a peasant."

"Tomorrow!" Lobelia gasped. "We don't have a moment to lose! Kneel down, Wiglaf. For you must kneel when you first speak to the princess."

Wiglaf fell to his knees.

"Start by praising Belcheena," Lobelia said. "Tell her she has lovely eyes and hair and lips. Make your bride-to-be feel beautiful!"

"Uh...beautiful Belcheena," Wiglaf began. "You have hair. And...uh, teeth..."

"Oh, for goodness' sakes!" Mordred cried. "Like this!" The big man dropped to his knees. He clasped his hands together. He blinked his violet eyes. "Oh, my lovely billionairess...er, I mean, princess!" he said. "Your hair shines like pure gold in the sunlight. Your eyes are as blue as sapphires! Your teeth are as bright as freshly minted coins!"

Wiglaf tried again. "Oh, Princess, your skin is as soft...as...as a sheep's belly."

"Not a sheep's belly!" Mordred bellowed.

"A sheep's belly *is* very soft," Wiglaf said.

"But not terribly romantic," Lobelia pointed out. "Say soft as a cloud."

After the praising lesson, Lobelia sat Wiglaf down. He practiced keeping his elbows off the table. He practiced drinking from a goblet without slurping. All the while, Lobelia read to him from *Medieval Manners: Do's and Don't's*.

"'Don't spit in your plate during dinner,'"

she read. "'Wait until the meal is finished. Don't pick your teeth with your knife—always use the point of your sword. Don't blow your nose on the hem of the tablecloth. Use your sleeve.'"

Lobelia kept at it all morning. She dismissed Wiglaf for lunch, telling him to practice his manners in the dining hall. Wiglaf's head spun with do's and don't's as he carried his tray to the Class I table.

"Wiglaf!" Erica exclaimed as he sat down. "I have good news!"

"What?" Wiglaf's heart leapt with hope. "Has Yorick returned with an answer from Belcheena?"

"No. But my order from *The Sir Lancelot Catalog* came!" Erica announced.

Wiglaf's heart sank. "That's nice," he managed.

"Here," Erica said. "I want you to have this." She pressed a ring into his hand. It had a milky blue stone. "It's a Sir Lancelot almost-magic foretelling ring," she explained. "When the stone is blue, all is well. But if it turns orange and starts blinking, it means *danger, danger, danger!*"

Wiglaf slipped the ring onto the first finger of his left hand. The stone's blue glow comforted him somehow. He thanked Erica.

"After lunch, let's go find Yorick," Angus suggested. "Maybe he has brought back Belcheena's reply. And surely that will be good news."

They found Yorick outside the henhouse. He was gathering feathers for his pigeon disguise.

"Yorick!" Wiglaf called. "Did you give Princess Belcheena the letter?"

"Uh...thieves set upon me!" Yorick cried.

"Didn't you squat down on the side of the road and pretend to be a rock?" Angus asked.

"Of course I did!" Yorick said. "But the

thieves thought I *was* a rock. So they sat on me! I let out a cry. And the next thing I knew, they were robbing me! Took my penny, they did. So here." Yorick pulled the letter from his tunic and gave it to Wiglaf. "I knew you wouldn't want me delivering it without my proper pay."

Wiglaf groaned. Here was his last chance to keep Belcheena from coming to DSA—ruined! He crumpled the letter into a ball.

Erica patted Wiglaf on the back. "Don't worry, Wiggie," she said. "Look. Your ring is still blue. There is no danger. Everything will turn out all right. Come! Let us be off to Slaying Class. Sir Mort is teaching us today."

"I shall be there in a minute," Wiglaf told his friends. "First I must go see Daisy."

Wiglaf walked to the henhouse.

"Daisy?" he called. "Are you here, girl?"

Daisy came trotting out to meet Wiglaf.

"Ello-hay, Iggie-way!" she exclaimed.

Wiglaf knelt down. He put his arms around his pig and hugged her.

"I can't stay long, Daisy," he said. "But I had to see you. For alas! Mordred is trying to make me get mar...mar..." No sound came out. But he managed to mouth the word.

Daisy gasped. "Arried-may?"

Wiglaf nodded. Then he poured his heart out to his pig. "I even tried to get out of it by saying that you must be in the wedding," Wiglaf added.

"Eally-ray?" Daisy said brightly.

Wiglaf nodded. "But Lobelia liked the idea! She wants you to be the flower pig!"

"I-yay ould-way ove-lay o-tay!" Daisy said.

"No, no!" Wiglaf cried. "I don't want to get mar... I want things to stay just as they are!"

"Illy-say oy-bay!" Daisy exclaimed. "I-yay ove-lay eddings-way!"

Wiglaf moaned. Daisy didn't seem to understand. He had counted on his wise pig to help him. He had never guessed that Daisy was so very fond of weddings.

"E-may, a-yay ower-flay ig-pay!" Daisy burbled happily. "Is-thay is-yay e-thay appiest-hay ay-day of-yay y-may ife-lay!"

"I must go to Slaying, Daisy." Wiglaf stood up. He rubbed his pig on her head. Then he stumbled from the henhouse in a daze.

Slaying Class went badly for Wiglaf that afternoon. He was late, for one thing. And he never had gotten the homework from Torblad. Sir Mort called on him to name three spots on a dragon where a dragon slayer could strike a fatal blow. But he could not name even one. The old knight looked very disappointed.

When at last class ended, Wiglaf ran over to Angus and Erica.

"I have an idea," he whispered to them. "For getting out of getting mar...mar... For getting out of this mess. I shall call Zelnoc!"

"That crazy wizard?" Angus asked. "The one who messed up Daisy's speech spell?"

"He's not very good," Wiglaf admitted. "But he *is* a wizard. Surely he must have some magic that can help me."

"We have a break before Alchemy Class," Erica said. "Let us summon this enchanter now."

"I know a secret part of the dungeon," Angus added. "No one ever goes there."

"Perfect," Wiglaf said. "Let's go there now. For my time is running out!"

Chapter 6

iglaf, Angus, and Erica ran down the stone stairway to the dungeon. Angus led them to a damp room way at the back. A tiny window near the ceiling let in the only light.

Wiglaf closed his eyes. He chanted Zelnoc's name backwards three times: "Conlez, Conlez, Conlez."

A faint breeze tickled Wiglaf's cheek. He opened his eyes. A puff of smoke was rising from the floor. The puff grew and grew until the room was filled with thick black smoke.

Wiglaf's eyes began to water.

Angus and Erica started coughing.

Then suddenly, out of the smoke, leapt a

white rabbit. It was followed by another. And another. Before long, dozens of the furry creatures were hopping around the dungeon.

"Zelnoc?" Wiglaf called. "Are you here?"

"Of course I am!" boomed a voice inside the smoke. "I was summoned, was I not?"

With that, the smoke lifted. And there stood a wizard. He wore a dark blue pointed hat and robe, dotted with silver stars.

"Whoa!" Angus said. He and Erica backed up.

Zelnoc stepped forward, tripping over a rabbit.

"Blasted bunnies!" he cursed. "How was I to know that saying *Bibbity Babbit* summoned rabbits? I thought I was doing a wart removal chant. So, it's you, is it, Weglip?"

"Yes, sir." Wiglaf began to worry. He had forgotten how mixed up Zelnoc's spells could get. "These are my friends, Eric and Angus."

"Charmed," Zelnoc said. "Do either of you know a spell for getting rid of rabbits?"

Erica and Angus shook their heads.

"I didn't think so," Zelnoc said miserably. He turned to Wiglaf. "So, what'll it be this time, Wigloaf? Another courage spell?"

"No, sir," Wiglaf said. "I need a spell so I won't have to get mar...mar..."

"Married," Angus put in. "My Uncle Mordred is arranging for him to marry Princess Belcheena."

"A princess, eh?" Zelnoc exclaimed. "Good work, my boy! Princesses don't usually go for you peasant types."

"I don't want her to go for me," Wiglaf exclaimed. "I called you to get me out of it!"

"No problem," Zelnoc said. "I'll brew you an anti-love potion. Belcheena takes a few sips of it and—zowie! The first person she lays eyes on, she shall hate with all her might."

"That sounds perfect!" Wiglaf said. "And I shall make certain that person is *me!*"

"Tell me, wizard," Erica said. "What do you put into such a potion?"

"A pinch of pepper, six hairs from a skunk tail, a lump of lumpen pudding," Zelnoc said. "I can't tell the whole recipe, of course. That would be breaking Wizard Rule #457. But it's a doozie."

"When can I have it?" Wiglaf asked.

"Let me think...." The wizard tapped his fingers on his chin. "Two weeks from today."

"Alas!" Wiglaf cried. "Then I am doomed!"

"The wedding is to take place next Saturday," Angus explained.

"Why didn't you say it was a rush job?" asked Zelnoc. "Nothing is impossible! We wizards always have a trick up our sleeves!"

To prove his point, Zelnoc reached up his sleeve. He pulled out...a rabbit.

"Egad!" he cried as the bunny jumped from his hand. "I'm having a really bad hare day!"

"Is there nothing else you can do for Wiglaf, sir?" asked Erica.

"There is always something else," Zelnoc said. "I'll give Waglom a smelling spell. It's like perfume—with a kick. Let me see.... Ah! I know! Whiff of Loathing. That's the ticket. One sniff, and bingo! Belcheena will detest you forever! Or at least until the spell wears off. Never fear! I shall bring it soon. Now, I must get back to my tower and figure out how to get rid of these rabbits."

"Oh, thank you, sir!" Wiglaf said, as, once more, the dungeon filled with smoke.

"Farewell, Wugloom!" Zelnoc called. "Come, bunnies! Hop to it!"

The rabbits jumped into the smoke with Zelnoc. Then, one and all, they disappeared.

Wiglaf ran happily up the dungeon stairs after Erica and Angus. Summoning Zelnoc had been a good idea after all! At the top of the stairs, they bumped into Mordred.

"Wiglaf!" the headmaster boomed. "I've been looking for you." He sniffed. "Do I smell smoke?"

"Frypot must have burned the lumpen pudding again," Angus said quickly.

"Ah, yes," Mordred said. "Come, Wiglaf! Lobelia is waiting!"

"But sir!" Wiglaf said. "I have to go to Alchemy Class."

"Classes are canceled," Mordred said. "Except for Scrubbing. Eric and Angus, you missed the sign-up. So you'll have to scrub the privy. Wiglaf, you go to Lobelia's. She's waiting to give you a makeover."

"A...what?" Wiglaf said.

"Lobelia wants you to look your best when you meet Belcheena tomorrow," Mordred said. "So go!"

Wiglaf hurried down the hallway. To his

horror, he saw that the stone in his ring was turning orange. It started blinking: *danger, danger, danger!* His heart pounded. This was not a good sign.

"Wiglaf!" Lobelia exclaimed as she waved him into her chamber. "I found the most charming drawing of Prince Putroc in *Royal Lads Magazine*. Just feast your eyes on his hair!" Lobelia held up the drawing. Prince Putroc's hair hung down on his forehead in ringlet curls. "You, Wiglaf, will look royal when I've curled your hair."

"*My* hair?" Wiglaf cried. No wonder his ring had been blinking! "No! Please! That picture is...awful!"

"Trust me on this, Wiglaf," Lobelia said. "Those curls are *you!* But we have a few other things to take care of first. Sit on that stool."

Wiglaf sat. Lobelia began spreading foul-smelling green goo all over his face.

"This clay is from Dead Fish Swamp. It does wonders for the skin. There." She stepped back to see if she had missed any spots.

Wiglaf felt the clay hardening.

"Now tilt your head back," Lobelia said.

Wiglaf did as he was told.

"Cucumbers take away puffiness." She pressed two big slices over his eyes.

Wiglaf felt the juice trickling into his ears.

"And for your lips," Lobelia added, "pepper paste." She smeared some on.

"Yow!" Wiglaf yelped. "It stings!"

"That's what brings out the nice rosy color," Lobelia explained. "Try not to lick your lips."

Wiglaf wanted to ask how long he must have all this disgusting stuff on him. But he was afraid to open his mouth.

"You know your ears stick out, don't you, Wiglaf?" Lobelia went on. "Well, I'm told that half an onion will draw the ear closer to the head." She hung half an onion from a string on each of Wiglaf's ears.

"Now hold still while I work on your fingernails," Lobelia said. "Rough hands are the sign of a peasant. Maybe you should wear gloves."

When she finished his nails, Lobelia began wrapping strands of Wiglaf's hair around a red-hot curling iron.

Wiglaf had faced two fire-breathing dragons. They had not killed him. But he thought Lobelia might. Certainly she was skilled at torture.

It seemed to Wiglaf that his makeover took forever. But at last he found his way back to the dorm room. He had a nasty rash on his cheeks from the swamp clay. His lips burned a fiery red. Carrot-colored ringlets danced on his forehead.

"Wiglaf!" Erica exclaimed when she saw him. "Have you caught the plague?"

"I wish," Wiglaf moaned. "Death by plague must be better than a makeover!" He flopped down on his cot. "And the worst is yet to come. Belcheena arrives tomorrow."

"We have to help him, Angus," Erica said.

"We do," Angus agreed. "But how?"

"How indeed." Erica tapped her foot as she thought. "I do have one idea," she said at last. "The Bag-o-Laughs Kit I ordered from *Junior Jester Magazine*. That should do the trick!"

"Oh, I think I saw some of the stuff you got...like the flower that squirts water?" Angus said. "And the black gum that makes one's teeth appear to be missing? And the hand buzzer? And the fake doggie poo?"

"Yes!" Erica answered with a smile. "We shall give Belcheena a very special welcome indeed!"

Chapter 7

On Saturday morning, Wiglaf opened his eyes. He checked his ring. It was blue now. But surely it would soon turn orange. For this was the day Belcheena was coming!

After breakfast, Wiglaf slowly made his way to Lobelia's chamber. He had just raised his hand to knock on the door, when a bright light flashed before him.

"Egad!" cried Wiglaf, jumping back.

In the spot where the light had been, Zelnoc shimmered into being.

"How do you like my new entrance?" the wizard asked. "I call it 'The Flash.' Beats the smoke, yes sir! I'm on a roll now, Waglop! I invented Bunnies-B-Gone. And poof! No more rabbits!"

"That's nice," Wiglaf said. "Did you bring me the loathing stuff?"

"Do bats have wings?" the wizard said. "Of course I did!" He reached up his sleeve and pulled out a bottle of bright red liquid.

"Are you sure it will work?" Wiglaf asked.

Zelnoc scowled down at Wiglaf. "Would I bring you something that didn't work?"

"Well..." Wiglaf didn't know how to put it. Zelnoc's spells had a way of turning out badly.

Just then, Lobelia opened her door.

"Hello, Wiglaf," she said. Then she looked at Zelnoc. "A wizard!" she exclaimed. "But why are you dressed in that old robe?"

Zelnoc frowned. "What's wrong with it?"

"That star pattern is *so* last year," Lobelia said. "Wizards nowadays go in for comets, meteor showers, shooting stars. They want a

powerful image. But come in, both of you."
She smiled. "I have a surprise for Wiglaf."

A surprise? Wiglaf had had more than
enough of those. But he followed Zelnoc into
Lobelia's chamber. And there was Daisy.

Wiglaf stared. His pig wore a pink silk cape.
A crown of tiny rosebuds sat on her head.

"Why are you dressed up?" Zelnoc asked.

"Iglaf-way's edding-way," Daisy said.

"Ah, yes. The wedding." Zelnoc winked at
Wiglaf. "That's why I'm here, too, in a way."

Lobelia gasped. "Wiglaf, that's brilliant!"
she cried. "A wizard in your wedding!"

"No, no, no," Zelnoc said. "Wizard Rule
#45 clearly states *no wizards in weddings*.
Funerals, sometimes. But weddings? Never."

"Oh, rules were made to be broken,"
Lobelia scoffed. She began circling Zelnoc.
"I'll trim your beard and find you a new robe.
One that will make you *look* powerful, even if
your powers aren't up to scratch."

"What?" Zelnoc cried. "My powers are just fine, thank you very much."

"Don't get huffy," Lobelia said.

"Huffy?" Zelnoc exclaimed. "Wizards don't get huffy! Wizards get *angry!* Wizards get *even!* Especially mighty, powerful wizards, like me!"

"Oh, puh-leeze!" Lobelia exclaimed.

Zelnoc popped the cork on the bottle of red potion.

"Doubt my powers, will you?" Zelnoc snarled. "Well, let's have a little test."

He waved the bottle under Lobelia's nose.

Wiglaf watched in horror as Lobelia's violet eyes began rolling around in circles.

"What have you done?" Wiglaf cried.

Lobelia's eyes closed. Then they popped open. Lobelia stared at Zelnoc.

"Well?" the wizard said eagerly. "You hate me with all your heart, don't you?"

She clasped her hands to her chest and cried,

"Oh, say not such a cruel thing!
With love for you my heart does sing!"

"Uh-oh," said Zelnoc.

Lobelia went on:

"Your wizard's hat is such a tall one!
In love with you I must have fallen!"

"E-shay oves-lay ou-yay!" Daisy sang happily.

"This is worse than rabbits!" Zelnoc cried.

Lobelia continued:

"Oh, Wizard, though you're old and wrinkled,
With love for you my heart is sprinkled!"

Wiglaf grabbed the bottle of red liquid from Zelnoc's hand. He read the tiny printing on the label: "Oil of Rhymes-o-Love."

"Oops," Zelnoc said. "I picked up the wrong bottle. But it works, Wuglop. You can see that, can't you? My spells do work!"

Lobelia took Zelnoc's hand in hers.

"Wizard, with your beard so white!
Dance with me in the pale moonlight!"

Zelnoc pulled his hand away. "Wizard Rule #498—*no dancing*. I'm getting out of here!"

Lobelia cried,

"Oh, wizard, with your robe so blue,
If you leave, I'll cry: Boo hoo!"

Zelnoc turned to Wiglaf. "I'm gone," he said. And with a bright flash of light, he was.

Tears streamed down Lobelia's cheeks.

"My wizard, he is gone from me.
I cannot stand such misery!"

"You don't really love him, my lady," Wiglaf said weakly. "It's a spell. It will wear off."

But Lobelia would not be comforted. She cried and sobbed and carried on. At last she threw her velvet cloak around her shoulders.

"Where are you going?" Wiglaf asked.

Lobelia cried miserably:

"This pain I feel, I must be stopping!
There's just one cure—I'm going shopping!"

Chapter 8

iglaf sank onto Lobelia's couch. He should have known better than to call Zelnoc. Whiff of Loathing indeed!

"Oor-pay Obelia-lay!" Daisy exclaimed.

"Lobelia's spell will wear off," Wiglaf said. "But Belcheena will be mine forever!"

Mordred stuck his head in the door.

"Ah, here you are, Wiglaf!" he exclaimed. "Yorick has just spotted Princess Belcheena! She and her party are starting up Huntsman's Path. They will be here within the hour!"

"Woe is me!" Wiglaf groaned.

"Why are you not dressed?" Mordred asked. "And where is my sister?"

"Opping-shay," Daisy said.

"Shopping?" Mordred cried. "At a time like this? She must have gotten wind of that bodice sale over in Ratswhiskers. Well, never mind. Now where did she put that new outfit she ordered for you, Wiglaf? Ah, here it is!" Mordred picked up a package tied up with string. He thrust it into Wiglaf's hands.

Instantly, Wiglaf's ring begin to flash a bright orange warning.

"Go put it on!" Mordred roared.

Wiglaf shook as he ducked behind the tapestry. He was in danger! But what could he do? He took off his DSA uniform. He put on his new outfit.

"Don't dillydally, boy!" Mordred yelled.

Wiglaf quickly fastened the squirting flower that Erica had given him to the collar of his new tunic. He stuck the tooth-black gum into his pocket. He slipped the hand buzzer onto his palm. Then he stepped out from behind the tapestry.

Wiglaf yelped as he beheld himself in Lobelia's looking glass. No wonder his ring had signaled danger! For he wore a swamp-green velvet tunic. His skinny legs, in matching tights, looked like toothpicks. His shoes had long, curled-up toes!

Mordred set a swamp-green mushroom-shaped hat on top of Wiglaf's ringlets. "There!" he said. "The hat gives you a lordly look."

"Ery-vay oble-nay!" Daisy exclaimed.

Wiglaf didn't think "noble" was quite the right word. The right word was "ninny." He looked like some half-witted elf!

Wiglaf stared at himself. And then he smiled. Surely Princess Belcheena would never marry anyone who looked this foolish!

"Come!" Mordred said. "It is time for you to go to the castle yard to greet your bride!"

Wiglaf's shoes flapped as he followed Mordred outside.

Every DSA student stood in the castle yard, waiting to see the East Armpittsian princess.

Wiglaf heard giggles as he passed by.

"Look at mushroom head!" called a boy.

"Hey, string bean legs!" called another.

But Wiglaf walked with his head held high. So what if they laughed? If the silly outfit saved him from marrying Belcheena, he would gladly wear it for the rest of his life.

Wiglaf spotted Angus and Erica in the crowd. But he could only wave to them and walk on.

Suddenly trumpets sounded. And Yorick cried, "Her Royal Highness, Princess Belcheena!"

Then through the castle gates marched a juggler juggling oranges. He was followed by two jesters turning cartwheels. Three minstrels strolled in next, strumming their lutes and singing. Four ladies-in-waiting were followed by five servants. The last one held the leash of a fierce-looking wild boar with golden tips on his tusks.

Wiglaf had never seen such a glorious parade. If only he did not know who was at the end of it.

Now a team of six horses pulled a golden carriage through the gate. And waving from the window was none other than Princess Belcheena.

"Welcome to Dragon Slayers' Academy!" Mordred boomed. He nodded to the DSA band. The boys struck up a squeaky tune.

Wiglaf watched with growing dread as the servants opened the carriage door. The ladies-in-waiting helped Princess Belcheena out.

Belcheena was a large princess. Much larger than Wiglaf had expected. A pointed hat sat on her head. A long lacy scarf trailed down from its tip. Her braided yellow hair hung down nearly to her knees.

"Welcome, Princess!" Mordred said. "As headmaster of this fine academy, I welcome—"

"Stop!" Princess Belcheena cried.

Mordred stopped midspeech.

"Well, where is he?" the princess said loudly. "Where is this Wiglaf of Pinwick?"

"Right here, your loadedness!" Mordred said. "I mean, your loveliness! Go on, boy!" He gave Wiglaf a push. "Do as I taught you."

Wiglaf lurched forward.

"Look, Gretta," Belcheena said to the lady-in-waiting at her side. "His hair is not really red at all. I would call it orange."

Yes! Wiglaf thought. Belcheena wanted a truly redheaded husband. And he did not fill the bill!

"It is indeed orange," Wiglaf agreed.

To his surprise, the princess smiled. "My long-lost love had red-orange hair," she said. She plucked up a locket she wore on a chain around her neck. She opened it and sighed. "This is all I have left of him. A curl of his carroty hair!"

Wiglaf's face fell. This was not working out at all. She liked his stupid hair! But he wasn't giving up yet.

"Go on, Wiglaf. Compliment her," Mordred whispered.

Wiglaf stepped toward the princess.

"Beautiful Belcheena," he said. "You smell as sweet as the flower I wear on my tunic!"

Belcheena leaned forward to smell the flower. Wiglaf pushed a little bulb in his pocket. *Spuuuurt!* The flower squirted Belcheena's face.

"Aaack!" cried the surprised princess.

"My lady!" screamed Gretta. She began patting Belcheena's cheeks dry with her handkerchief.

Before the princess could recover, Wiglaf struck again. "Princess Belcheena," he said. "Let me kiss your hand!"

He took Belcheena's hand in his and squeezed.

The hand buzzer sounded: *Buzzzzzzzzzz!*

"Yowie!" Belcheena cried. She jumped back.

Mordred rushed over to Belcheena.

"Princess!" he cried. "I shall have Wiglaf flogged! I'll put him in the Thumb Screws. I'll put him in the Foot Smasher. I'll put him in the Limb Stretcher until his arms are six feet long!"

"Shush!" Belcheena waved Mordred away. She eyed Wiglaf. "I was not expecting that!" she said.

Wiglaf smiled broadly.

"Please forgive Wiglaf, Princess!" Mordred cried. "I shall throw him in the dungeon! But of course, you will still marry him, won't you? You'll still give me that great big pot of gold?"

"Scat!" Belcheena yelled at Mordred.

The headmaster slunk away.

"Tell me, Wiglaf of Pinwick!" Belcheena said. "The squirting flower and the hand buzzer...are they from the Junior Jester Bag-o-Laughs Kit?"

The question caught Wiglaf by surprise.

"Why, yes, they are, my lady," he answered.

"Ha!" Belcheena cried. She gave Wiglaf a hearty slap on the back. "There's nothing I like better than a practical joke!" She grinned. "I, too, ordered the Bag-o-Laughs! I was going to have some fun with you! Just look!"

Belcheena slipped her hand into the pocket of her gown. She brought her hand to her mouth. Then she smiled, and her two front teeth appeared to be missing.

Belcheena threw back her head and roared with laughter. She gave Wiglaf another mighty slap. This one sent him sprawling face-down in the castle yard.

"You are not half the man my long-lost love was," the princess said as Wiglaf struggled to his feet. "Not even a quarter, really. But you're a rascal! Oh, what fine times we shall have at Mildew Palace!"

"You...you like him then?" Mordred asked. "You still want to marry Wiglaf?"

"Why not?" Belcheena boomed. "And why wait a week? Let us be wed tomorrow!"

"But...but...but..." Wiglaf sputtered.

He was drowned out by Mordred. "Oh, joy! Oh, golden day!" the headmaster cried. "By the way, your royal richness. I mean, highness...about that pot of gold."

Princess Belcheena rolled her eyes. "Is that all you can think of?" she asked.

"Well, frankly...yes," Mordred mumbled. "I mean, no! Of course not!"

"Good," said the princess. "Now, I have had

a hard journey to this forsaken part of the kingdom. I want to rest. Is your very best room ready for me?"

"Yes, Princess!" Mordred said. "Yorick!" he called. "Show the princess to her room!"

"Ta ta, Wigs!" Belcheena wiggled her fingers at him. "Wait! What is that on your head?"

"What?" said Wiglaf. He swatted at his hair.

"This." Belcheena reached out and seemed to pluck something from the top of his head. She held it out in front of him.

It was a...a human thumb! Blood was caked around its base where it had been cut from a hand! Wiglaf swayed dizzily, just looking at it.

"Ha!" Belcheena cackled. "Gotcha, Wigs!"

She tossed the horrid thumb to him. It was made of rubber. Then she skipped merrily into the castle.

"Back to class, boys!" Mordred cried. "We'll celebrate tonight at Wiglaf's bachelor party!"

"Hooray!" the students cheered.

Angus and Erica ran over to Wiglaf. "I'm doomed!" Wiglaf cried.

"No, you're not," Erica said. "Look at your ring. The stone is still blue."

But Wiglaf was losing faith in his ring. "Here," he said, handing the thumb to Erica.

"Thanks!" Erica exclaimed. "The severed thumb only comes in the super-duper Bag-o-Laughs. You get a whoopie cushion with that one, too."

"That's nice," said Wiglaf. But he wasn't thinking about whoopie cushions. Or severed thumbs. He was thinking of Princess Belcheena. And how he was going to be spending the rest of his life with her.

Chapter 9

"Three cheers for the groom!" Mordred boomed as Wiglaf walked into the dining hall for his bachelor party that night.

"Hip, hip, hooray!" everyone cried three times.

The room was hung with greenery. Platters of steaming food lined the tables. There wasn't a bowl of lumpen pudding in sight.

Wiglaf sat in the seat of honor. Angus and Erica sat on either side of him. They dug into the dinner. But Wiglaf could not eat a bite.

Mordred strolled by. "Eat up, Wiglaf!" he roared. "I've spared no expense. Ah, what fun it is to spend the princess's money!" He clapped

Wiglaf on the back. "Have you picked a best man yet, my boy?"

Wiglaf turned to Angus. "Would you?" he asked.

"Honored," Angus said, with his mouth full.

During dinner, the juggler juggled. The minstrels sang. The boar was led around the room so that all might admire his fine gold-tipped tusks. Wiglaf would have enjoyed himself tremendously if only there had been another reason for the party.

Coach Plungett stood up to give a toast. He raised his flask. "Word reached me at my mother's cottage in Ratswhiskers that you were getting married, Wiglaf," he said. "I rushed back to wish you all the happiness in the world! Love is a wonderful thing, lad. Why, thinking of my long-lost lady love still makes my heart beat with joy. Some would say that I have been unlucky in love. Yet I say—not so! For a while, my lady love and I were as happy as pigs in a mud wallow. I remember the time..."

"Give your toast and sit down, Wendell!" Frypot called. "We don't want to be here all night!"

"To Wiglaf and his bride!" Coach said.

"Here! Here!" everyone shouted. "To Wiglaf and Belcheena!"

"Belcheena?" Suddenly, Coach choked on his mead and started coughing. Mordred had to slap him on the back for quite a while before the big man recovered.

Brother Dave gave the last toast of the evening. "Sleep well tonight, Wiglaf," the monk said. "For tomorrow when thou hearest wedding bells, they shall be ringing for thee!"

"I...I do," Wiglaf stuttered. He stood just

inside the door of the DSA castle, between his best man Angus and Mordred.

"Louder!" Mordred barked.

"I do!" Wiglaf shouted miserably.

Angus patted his shoulder.

The wedding was about to begin. Wiglaf pulled the scratchy pleated white collar away from his neck. Why did he have to wear the silly thing? Wasn't he in enough pain already?

A wedding day was supposed to be a happy day. But Wiglaf felt like crying. He did not want to leave his friends. He did not want to live in Mildew Palace with that prankster Belcheena. He did not even want to help her spend her billions.

"Once more," Mordred commanded.

"I dooooo!" wailed Wiglaf.

"That's better!" Mordred said.

Suddenly Lobelia rushed into the castle. She was loaded down with shopping bags.

"Oh, thank goodness!" she cried. "I made it back in time. I don't know what came over me, rushing off like that. Mordie, go check on Dr. Pluck. Tell him to start playing the organ!"

Mordred hurried off.

Lobelia uncapped a bottle from one of her bags. She squirted a sweet-smelling liquid on Wiglaf. "It's Groom Perfume," she said. "Isn't it wild? I'd better check on the bridesmaids now. I'll be back." And off she rushed.

Yuck! Now Wiglaf smelled just like a rose! He peeked out the door at Lobelia's rose-bushes. They were in full bloom. A cloth runner had been put down on the grass for Belcheena to walk on. Class III students were seating the wedding guests on long wooden benches.

Suddenly organ music started playing. Yikes! The wedding had begun!

Brother Dave walked out of the chapel. He stopped between the two biggest rosebushes.

"That is our signal," Angus whispered.

Wiglaf stood rooted to the spot.

"Come on!" Angus said. And he pulled the reluctant groom out into the castle yard.

Wiglaf blinked in the sunlight. He walked toward Brother Dave.

"Thou art doing fine, lad," the monk said when Wiglaf reached him.

Next came the wedding party, Gretta and the other ladies-in-waiting, with Daisy trotting behind them. She was wearing her pink silk cape. And her crown of rosebuds.

People gasped when they saw Daisy. They murmured to each other "Pig in a wedding!" and "What next?"

Now Dr. Pluck pounded on the organ keys and struck up "Here Comes the Bride."

Sir Mort began escorting Belcheena up the

runner. The princess wore a red gown. Her yellow braids were wound with ropes of pearls.

"So beautiful!" whispered the wedding guests. "Such a lovely dress!"

Wiglaf swallowed as the princess walked closer and closer to him. Her lips were bright pink. Her cheeks were rouged red. Blue shadow lined her eyelids. Wiglaf thought she looked scarier than any dragon.

Wiglaf found Erica's face in the crowd. She held up a finger. Wiglaf understood. He looked down at his ring. The stone was bright blue.

Phooey! he thought. The thing ought to be glowing like a red-hot coal! Clearly, *The Sir Lancelot Catalog* had sold Erica a dud.

Sir Mort walked Belcheena to her groom. He put the princess's arm on Wiglaf's. Then he bowed and took a seat in the front row beside Mordred.

Belcheena winked and smiled at Wiglaf.

Wiglaf tried to smile back.

"Dearly beloved," Brother Dave began. "We have come here today to join Belcheena Kristen Louise Wilhemina Bernadette Paula Frieda Marie, Princess of East Armpittsia and Wiglaf of Pinwick in marriage."

Wiglaf's knees began to shake.

"Steady, Wiglaf," Angus whispered.

"If any persons here know of a reason why these two people should not be joined in marriage," Brother Dave went on, "let them speak now, or forever hold their peace."

Silence filled the castle yard.

Brother Dave turned to Belcheena.

"Princess Belcheena," he said. "Do you take this—"

"Stop!" called a voice from the gatehouse. "Stop the wedding now!"

Chapter 10

he wedding guests gasped.

Wiglaf whirled around. His eyes searched the crowd.

"Look, there." Angus pointed toward the gatehouse. A tall man was making his way through the crowd.

Wiglaf gasped. "It's Coach Plungett!"

What is going on? he wondered.

Suddenly Belcheena let out a scream.

Wiglaf jumped.

Was this another one of Belcheena's jokes?

"Wendell!" Belcheena called. "Is it you?"

"Yes, Belchie? It is!" Coach Plungett cried. He ran up to the princess. Belcheena slowly held out her hand. Coach reached for it. But the princess quickly drew her hand away. "Gotcha!" she shrieked.

"Whoo-whoo!" Coach Plungett cried. "It's my rowdy old Belchie!" Then he picked her up and whirled her around and around.

"STOP THAT!" Mordred boomed.

Coach put the princess down.

"What, in the name of King Ken's britches, are you doing, Plungett?" Mordred roared.

"Gazing at my long-lost love," Coach replied. "Dearest Belchie!" he said. "I thought never to see you again!"

"Why did you leave me, Wendell? Why?" Belcheena asked.

"Your father's henchmen drove me from your palace," Coach Plungett said. "Many times I tried to return. But the guards kept me out. At last I went off questing in the Dark Forest. I tried to forget you, Belchie. But I never could."

"I never forgot you either," Belcheena said. "After you left, all I did was count my gold, order silly things from *Junior Jester Magazine*, and sing this song. Listen." And Belcheena began to sing.

> *"He set my heart on fire,*
> *That's the truth, I am no liar.*
> *When he left I was a crier*
> *For the Squire of My Desire!*
>
> *"Throughout the whole empire*
> *He's the one that I admire.*
> *There is no squire higher*
> *Than the Squire of My Desire!"*

"Oh, Belchie!" cried Coach.

"Sit down, Plungett," Mordred ordered. "You and Belcheena can talk about old times later. Now, let's get back to the wedding!"

But the princess and the coach paid no attention to the headmaster.

"I shall not lose you again, Belchie!" Coach Plungett vowed. He dropped to his knees and said, "Will you marry me?"

The princess smiled. She turned to Wiglaf. "I hope you don't mind terribly," she said, "but I must marry Wendell."

"So you must, Princess," Wiglaf said happily. "You must marry the one you love."

There. He'd said it: Marry!

"What will your father say?" Coach asked.

"Who cares?" the princess replied.

"Hold it! Hold it!" Mordred cried. "What about your conditions, Your Highness? True, Wendell Plungett is a dragon slayer. And his first name begins with *W*. But," Mordred added slyly, "he does not have red hair!"

"'Tis true," Coach Plungett said. He pulled off his wig. "I no longer have *any* hair."

"Who cares?" Princess Belcheena said again. "You once had lovely carrot-colored hair. I still carry a curl of it in my locket. That is enough for me."

Mordred groaned.

"I'll be your best man, Coach," Wiglaf offered.

Brother Dave began again. "Dearly beloved, we have come here today to join Princess Belcheena of Mildew Palace, East Armpittsia, and Wendell Plungett of Dragon Slayers' Academy in marriage."

What a celebration followed! No one had a better time than Wiglaf. He cheered for the jugglers. He sang along with the minstrels. He danced with Daisy. Later he smiled when he saw his pig in the crowd, flirting with the golden-tusked boar. He'd never been so happy.

"Look," said Angus at last. "The bride and groom are getting into the carriage."

"Let us bid them good-bye," Erica said.

Wiglaf, Angus, and Erica hurried over.

"Farewell, Coach!" Wiglaf said. "Farewell, Princess Belcheena!"

"Good-bye!" Belcheena called. "Come and visit us at Mildew Palace, won't you, Wigs? And bring your friends."

Mordred pushed his way to the carriage. "Excuse me, Princess," he said. "But as your matchmaker, I was wondering.... About that pot of gold?"

"Ah!" Belcheena said. "But I have not married Wiglaf of Pinwick. So I owe you no pot of gold."

"But...but...but..." Mordred sputtered. "The price of the wedding supper alone..."

The princess reached out of the carriage and patted Mordred on the head. "Thanks for everything!" she exclaimed. Then the happy couple galloped off for their honeymoon.

"I'm ruined!" Mordred bellowed. "Ruined!"

He turned to Wiglaf, his violet eyes bulging. "It's all your fault!" he growled.

"*My* fault?" Wiglaf cried.

"If you weren't a redheaded dragon slayer named Wiglaf, none of this would have happened!" Mordred yelled. "I'm going to throw you into the dungeon. It's the Thumb Screws for you, my boy...."

The Sir Lancelot almost-magic ring began flashing a bright orange warning: *Danger, danger, danger!* Wiglaf didn't wait around to hear any more. He took off running. Angus and Erica took off after him. They knew just where to hide from Mordred until his temper cooled down—in the DSA library.

As Wiglaf ran, he felt better than he had felt in a long, long time. He felt as if he really might live happily ever after.

DSA
YEARBOOK

Goldius est goodius!

The Campus of Dragon Slayers' Academy

DSA

Lady Lobelia's Chamber

Dr. Pluck's Science Lab

Mordred's Classroom

Tunnel Exit

Headmaster's Office

Stab

Cast Yar

To Dungeon

Dining Hall

Scrubbing Class

Practi Drago

Yorick's Quick Change-O-Rama Camp Site

East Tower

Mort's
ist

Toenail Village

huntsman's
Path

Dormitory

Enter At Your Own Risk

DSA

Eels
Galore
Moat

Drawbridge

~ Our Founders ~

Sir Herbert Dungeonstone

Sir Ichabod Popquiz

~ Our Philosophy ~

Sir Herbert and Sir Ichabod founded
Dragon Slayers' Academy on a simple
principle still held dear today: Any lad—
no matter how weak, yellow-bellied, lazy,
pigeon-toed, smelly, or unwilling—can be
transformed into a fearless dragon slayer
who goes for the gold. After four years
at DSA, lads will finally be of some
worth to their parents, as well as a
source of great wealth to this distin-
guished academy.* ** ***

* Please note that Dragon Slayers' Academy is a strictly-for-profit
institution.

** Dragon Slayers' Academy reserves the right to keep some of the gold
and treasure that any student recovers from a dragon's lair.

*** The exact amount of treasure given to a student's family is deter-
mined solely by our esteemed headmaster, Mordred. The amount shall be
no less than 1/500th of the treasure and no greater than 1/499th.

Mordred de Marvelous

Mordred graduated from Dragon Bludgeon High, second in his class. The other student, Lionel Flyzwattar, went on to become headmaster of Dragon Stabbers' Prep. Mordred spent years as part-time, semi-substitute student teacher at Dragon Whackers' Alternative School, all the while pursuing his passion for mud wrestling. Inspired by how filthy rich Flyzwattar had become by running a school, Mordred founded Dragon Slayers' Academy in CMLXXIV, and has served as headmaster ever since.

❦

Known to the Boys as: Mordred de Miser
Dream: Piles and piles of dragon gold
Reality: Yet to see a single gold coin
Best-Kept Secret: Mud wrestled under the name Macho-Man Mordie
Plans for the Future: Will retire to the Bahamas . . . as soon as he gets his hands on a hoard

Lady Lobelia

Lobelia de Marvelous is Mordred's sister and a graduate of the exclusive If-You-Can-Read-This-You-Can-Design-Clothes Fashion School. Lobelia has offered fashion advice to the likes of King Felix the Husky and Eric the Terrible Dresser. In CMLXXIX, Lobelia married the oldest living knight, Sir Jeffrey Scabpicker III. That's when she gained the title of Lady Lobelia, but—alas!—only a very small fortune, which she wiped out in a single wild shopping spree. Lady Lobelia has graced Dragon Slayers' Academy with many visits, and can be heard around campus saying, "Just because I live in the Middle Ages doesn't mean I have to look middle-aged."

⚜

Known to the Boys as: Lady Lo Lo
Dream: Frightfully fashionable
Reality: Frightful
Best-Kept Secret: Shops at Dark-Age Discount Dress Dungeon
Plans for the Future: New uniforms for the boys with mesh tights and lace tunics

Sir Mort du Mort

Sir Mort is our well-loved professor of Dragon Slaying for Beginners as well as Intermediate and Advanced Dragon Slaying. Sir Mort says that, in his youth, he was known as the Scourge of Dragons. (We're not sure what it means, but it sounds scary.) His last encounter was with the most dangerous dragon of them all: Knight-shredder. Early in the battle, Sir Mort took a nasty blow to his helmet and has never been the same since.

�֍

Known to the Boys as: The Old Geezer
Dream: Outstanding Dragon Slayer
Reality: Just plain out of it
Best-Kept Secret: He can't remember
Plans for the Future: Taking a little nap

~ Faculty ~

Coach Wendell Plungett

Coach Plungett spent many years questing in the Dark Forest before joining the Athletic Department at DSA. When at last he strode out of the forest, leaving his dragon-slaying days behind him, Coach Plungett was the most muscle-bulging, physically fit, manliest man to be found anywhere north of Nowhere Swamp. "I am what you call a hunk," the coach admits. At DSA, Plungett wears a number of hats—or, helmets. Besides PE Teacher, he is Slaying Coach, Square-Dance Director, Pep-Squad Sponsor, and Privy Inspector. He hopes to meet a damsel—she needn't be in distress—with whom he can share his love of heavy metal music and long dinners by candlelight.

❧

Known to the Boys as: Coach
Dream: Tough as nails
Reality: Sleeps with a stuffed dragon named Foofoo
Best-Kept Secret: Just pull his hair
Plans for the Future: Finding his lost lady love

Brother Dave

Brother Dave is the DSA librarian. He belongs to the Little Brothers of the Peanut Brittle, an order known for doing impossibly good deeds and cooking up endless batches of sweet peanut candy. How exactly did Brother Dave wind up at Dragon Slayers' Academy? After a batch of his extra-crunchy peanut brittle left three children from Toenail toothless, Brother Dave vowed to do a truly impossible good deed. Thus did he offer to be librarian at a school world-famous for considering reading and writing a complete and utter waste of time. Brother Dave hopes to change all that.

❧

Known to the Boys as: Bro Dave
Dream: Boys reading in the libary
Reality: Boys sleeping in the library
Best-Kept Secret: Uses Cliff's Notes
Plans for the Future: Copying out all the lyrics to "Found a Peanut" for the boys

Professor Prissius Pluck

Professor Pluck graduated from Peter Piper Picked a Peck of Pickled Peppers Prep, and went on to become a professor of Science at Dragon Slayers' Academy. His specialty is the Multiple Choice Pop Test. The boys who take Dragon Science, Professor Pluck's popular class,

a) are amazed at the great quantities of saliva Professor P. can project

b) try never to sit in the front row

c) beg Headmaster Mordred to transfer them to another class

d) all of the above

⚜

Known to the Boys as: Old Spit Face

Dream: Proper pronunciation of *p*'s

Reality: Let us spray

Best-Kept Secret: Has never seen a pippi-hippo-pappa-peepus up close

Plans for the Future: Is working on a cure for chapped lips

Frypot

How Frypot came to be the cook at DSA is something of a mystery. Rumors abound. Some say that when Mordred bought the broken-down castle for his school, Frypot was already in the kitchen and he simply stayed on. Others say that Lady Lobelia hired Frypot because he was so speedy at washing dishes. Still others say Frypot knows many a dark secret that keeps him from losing his job. But no one ever, *ever* says that Frypot was hired because of his excellent cooking skills.

✤

Known to the Boys as: Who needs a nickname with a real name like Frypot?
Dream: Cleaner kitchen
Reality: Kitchen cleaner
Best-Kept Secret: Takes long bubble baths in the moat
Plans for the Future: Has signed up for a beginning cooking class

Yorick

Yorick is Chief Scout at DSA. His knack for masquerading as almost anything comes from his years with the Merry Minstrels and Dancing Damsels Players, where he won an award for his role as the Glass Slipper in "Cinderella". However, when he was passed over for the part of Mama Bear in "Goldilocks", Yorick decided to seek a new way of life. He snuck off in the night and, by dawn, still dressed in the bear suit,

found himself walking up Huntsmans Path. Mordred spied him from a castle window, recognized his talent for disguise, and hired him as Chief Scout on the spot.

❧

Known to the Boys as: Who's that?
Dream: Master of Disguise
Reality: Mordred's Errand Boy
Best-Kept Secret: Likes dressing up as King Ken
Plans for the Future: To lose the bunny suit

Wiglaf of Pinwick

Wiglaf, our newest lad, hails from a hovel outside the village of Pinwick, which makes Toenail look like a thriving metropolis. Being one of thirteen children, Wiglaf had a taste of dorm life before coming to DSA and he fit right in. He started the year off with a bang when he took a stab at Coach Plungett's brown pageboy wig. Way to go, Wiggie! We hope to see more of this lad's wacky humor in the years to come.

✤

Dream: Bold Dragon-Slaying Hero
Reality: Still hangs on to a "security" rag
Extracurricular Activities: Animal-Lovers Club, President; No More Eel for Lunch Club, President; Frypot's Scrub Team, Brush Wielder; Pig Appreciation Club, Founder
Favorite Subject: Library
Oft-Heard Saying: *"Ello-hay, Aisy-day!"*
Plans for the Future: To go for the gold!

Angus du Pangus

The nephew of Mordred and Lady Lobelia, Angus walks the line between saying, "I'm just one of the lads" and "I'm going to tell my uncle!" Will this Class I lad ever become a mighty dragon slayer? Or will he take over the kitchen from Frypot some day? We of the DSA Yearbook staff are betting on choice #2. And hey, Angus? The sooner the better!

⚜

Dream: A wider menu selection at DSA
Reality: Eel, Eel, Eel!
Extracurricular Activities: DSA Cooking Club, President; Smilin' Hal's Off -Campus Eatery, Sales Representative
Favorite Subject: Lunch
Oft-Heard Saying: *"I'm still hungry"*
Plans for the Future: To write *101 Ways to Cook a Dragon*

Eric von Royale

Eric hails from Someplace Far Away (at least that's what he wrote on his Application Form). There's an air of mystery about this Class I lad, who says he is "totally typical and absolutely average." If that is so, how did he come to own the rich tapestry that hangs over his cot? And are his parents really close personal friends of Sir Lancelot? Did Frypot the cook bribe him to start the Clean Plate Club? And doesn't Eric's arm ever get tired from raising his hand in class so often?

⚜

Dream: Valiant Dragon Slayer
Reality: Teacher's Pet
Extracurricular Activities: Sir Lancelot Fan Club; Armor Polishing Club; Future Dragon Slayer of the Month Club; DSA Pep Squad, Founder and Cheer Composer
Favorite Subject: All of Them!!!!!
Oft-Heard Saying: *"When I am a mighty Dragon Slayer . . ."*
Plans for the Future: To take over DSA

Baldrick de Bold

This is a banner year for Baldrick. He is celebrating his tenth year as a Class I lad at DSA. Way to go, Baldrick! If any of you new students want to know the ropes, Baldrick is the one to see. He can tell when you should definitely *not* eat the cafeteria's eel, where the choice seats are in Professor Pluck's class, and what to tell the headmaster if you are late to class. Just don't ask him the answer to any test questions.

⚜

Dream: To run the world
Reality: A runny nose
Extracurricular Activities: Practice Dragon Maintenance Squad; Least Improved Slayer-in-Training Award
Favorite Subject: *"Could you repeat the question?"*
Oft Heard Saying: *"A dragon ate my homework."*
Plans for the Future: To transfer to Dragon Stabbers' Prep

KNIGHT FOR A DAY

When Wiglaf learns that he has won "A Day
with Sir Lancelot (The World's Most Perfect Knight),"
he can hardly believe it. His friend Erica can't believe it,
either! And when the big day arrives, she is even more
doubtful. Is Erica just jealous, or is there something
fishy about The World's Most Perfect Knight?

OCT _ - 2012